Christmas
comes to
MOOMINVALLEY

This book belongs to:

....

Dear Reader,

The book that you hold in your hands is going to whisk you away on an amazing adventure with Moomintroll, his family and their friends in Moominvalley. This story is based on books written by my aunt Tove Jansson almost 75 years ago – books that your parents and their parents might even have read!

As a child I used to love listening to stories read aloud by grown-ups. What a wonderful feeling it was to sit curled up in the crook of someone's arm, listening to the story, looking at the pictures, and seeing new pictures drawn in my mind. It was my favourite part of the day, and it made me the book lover that I still am. I hope that these books will inspire the same feeling in you – we're off on an adventure to the magical world of Moominvalley, where absolutely anything can happen!

Sophia Jansson,
Tove Jansson's niece and
Creative Director of
Moomin Characters™

*Tove Jansson and some of
the inhabitants of Moominvalley*

Christmas comes to MOOMINVALLEY

Adapted from the *Tove Jansson* classic

ALEX HARIDI • CECILIA DAVIDSSON • FILIPPA WIDLUND

MACMILLAN CHILDREN'S BOOKS

Hattifatteners Island

Some of Moominvalley's inhabitants

Moomintroll *is curious and friendly. He loves going on adventures, especially if it means spending time with his friends. If ever the adventure becomes too scary, he always has his Moominmamma to come back to.*

Moominmamma *is soft in all the right places and has a handbag full of dry woolly socks, stomach powder and sweeties. She never loses her cool, and makes sure that every little creature in Moominvalley has a place to sleep if they need it.*

Moominpappa is a very well-travelled fellow, at least according to him. He often longs for wild adventures like the ones he experienced in his youth. Then he sits in his room and writes his memoirs, a long book about his great escapades.

Snorkmaiden loves everything that is beautiful, just like her. She is smart and inventive, but wishes that life in Moominvalley could be more grand and dramatic.

It was winter in Moominvalley. Under the ice, the
sea was silent and still. Under the ground, all the
little creepy-crawlies were curled up asleep.
And the Moomin family were cosy in bed, sleeping their
long winter sleep.

They had been asleep since October and planned to
continue until spring, as they did every year.

But the Hemulen didn't understand this.

He was standing on the roof, scrabbling through the thick snow until his woollen gloves became quite wet and unpleasant. He was searching for a roof hatch.

"Those trolls just sleep and sleep, and here I am working my tail off just because Christmas is coming," he muttered.

Finally he found the hatch. But he couldn't remember whether it opened inward or outward. He stamped on it, carefully. The hatch swung open and down tumbled the Hemulen, into the darkness.

"This is most un-Hemulenish!" exclaimed the Hemulen as he landed in a pile of clutter that the Moomin family were storing in the attic until spring.

Now he was well and truly annoyed. He stomped downstairs, threw open the door to the drawing room and shouted:

"Christmas is coming and here you are asleep! This won't do at all!"

A cold, troubling draught blew into Moomintroll's dreams. A heavy sigh came from deep beneath the blanket. The little troll wanted nothing more than to carry on sleeping and dreaming of sunny summer afternoons.

But alas he could not, for the Hemulen began yanking off his blanket and shouting at him to wake up.

"Is it spring already?" mumbled Moomintroll. "Is our sleep over?"

"Spring?" said the Hemulen. "Christmas is coming, don't you see, Christmas! I've so much to do, and on top of it all, they send me here to drag you out of bed. Everyone is rushed off their feet and nothing is ready. I've had quite enough of you and your sleeping!"

Then he stomped back upstairs and disappeared through the roof hatch.

"Mamma, wake up," said Moomintroll. "Something dreadful is coming! It's called Christmas."

"What's that?" said Moominmamma sleepily, poking her nose out from under her blanket.

"I'm not sure," said Moomintroll. "But the Hemulen says that nothing is ready and everyone is rushing about. Sounds like we ought to prepare."

Then he woke Snorkmaiden and whispered:

"Now don't be alarmed, but something dreadful is coming."

"Everybody stay calm," said Moominpappa. "We'll investigate the matter."

They followed the Hemulen's wet footprints up into the attic and climbed out onto the roof of Moominhouse.

But what was this?

The whole of Moominvalley was buried in wet
cotton wool. It covered the mountains and the
trees and the river and their entire house.
And it was cold.

"Is this Christmas?" asked
Moominpappa in astonishment. He
scooped up a pawful of cotton wool
and inspected it.

"I wonder if it grew out of the
ground. Or fell from the sky. It
must have hurt if it all came
falling down in one go," he said.
"Silly Pappa, it's snow! It
does fall from the sky, but
only a little at a time,"
said Moomintroll.

A friend of the Moomin family came by with a fir tree and noticed them sitting up on the roof.

"Oh, so you're finally awake. Better hurry if you're to get a fir tree before dark!" she called.

"A fir tree? Whatever for?" said Moominpappa.

But she hadn't the time to stay and talk more.

"She says we have to get a fir tree before dark!" whispered Snorkmaiden. "That means Christmas must be coming tonight . . ."

"And evidently one needs a fir tree to survive it," said Moominpappa. "What are we waiting for?"

"Put your scarves and gloves on before you go looking for a fir. Meanwhile I'll get a lovely fire going in the stove," said Moominmamma, who hated the thought of any living creature feeling cold. Little creatures like woodies, toffles and creeps, for example. One such pitiful creature was sitting under the verandah, shivering. She invited it inside at once for a nice hot cup of tea.

The others went into the forest to chop down a fir tree. But which should they choose? Perhaps Christmas demanded a certain type of fir tree?

"Do you suppose we're meant to hide in it?" wondered Moomintroll.

"I don't know," said Moominpappa. "I haven't the foggiest idea about any of this."

"If so, we had better get a big tree, so there's room enough for all of us," said Snorkmaiden.

"This will do," said Moominpappa and swung his axe at the nearest fir tree, which was not especially big. He was tired of looking. The snow was deep and his paws were cold.

"We can always squash together if need be," Pappa said – and he chopped down the tree.

They carried the fir tree home and planted it in
the snow.

"Well, here it is," said Moominpappa. "If only
we knew what to do with it."

"Wow-ee, it's beautiful!" exclaimed the little creature,
who had crept outside with Moominmamma. It blushed,
embarrassed to have said something out loud.

"Do you know what the fir tree is for?"
asked Moominpappa.

"You have to dress it," whispered the creature.

"Dress it? Our clothes aren't big enough,"
said Moominmamma.

"Not with clothes. With pretty things. The
prettiest things you have. Or so I heard . . ."

Then the little creature buried its face in its paws
and scuttled behind Moominmamma to hide.

Moominpappa thought about what the little creature
had said.

"I think I'm beginning to understand. If the idea is to
make the fir tree beautiful then it can't be a hiding place.
It must be a way to win over Christmas."

They started to dress the fir tree with beautiful things: shells, beads and crystals. At the top they put a red silk rose that Moominpappa had once given to Mamma. They dressed the tree with all the loveliest things they could find to appease the mysterious powers of winter.

"Perhaps Christmas won't be so terrible now," said Moomintroll.

Once they had finished decorating the tree, they saw a red figure approaching. It was Mrs Fillyjonk, in a frightful hurry.

"Look at our fir tree!" called Moomintroll.

"Me oh my, what a mess! But you always have been peculiar types. No time to stop . . . Must get the food ready for Christmas!" called Mrs Fillyjonk.

"Food for Christmas?" said Moomintroll. "Does it eat, too?"

"Goodness gracious! One simply must have food for Christmas," said Mrs Fillyjonk impatiently, as she sledged off down the hill.

Moominmamma rushed straight into the kitchen
and started bustling about. She made soured milk and
blueberry pie and eggnog and all manner of Moomin
family favourites.

"Do you think Christmas is very hungry?" she
asked worriedly.

"It can hardly be hungrier than I am," said Pappa,
looking longingly at all the delicious food.

Dusk was falling, and down in the valley candles were
starting to appear in all the windows. Lights twinkled
under the trees and from all the little nests in the branches.
Candlelight flickered and danced across the snow.

I suppose Christmas likes candles, thought Moomintroll.

Moomintroll gathered up all the candles he could find.
He stuck them in the snow around the fir tree and lit them,
one by one, until they were all burning bright to soften the
darkness – and Christmas.

The others served up the food into bowls.

All was quiet in Moominvalley. Everybody must have gone home to await the danger, thought Moomintroll. A lone figure came ambling through the trees. It was the Hemulen.

"Hello? Should we be expecting Christmas any time soon?" asked Moomintroll.

"Leave me alone," the Hemulen said grumpily and buried his nose in a great long list on which almost everything was crossed out. He muttered something about Christmas presents.

"What's the matter?" asked Snorkmaiden anxiously. "Has something happened?"

"Presents! More and more every year. How ever will I manage to get them all in time? I'm at my wits' end," the Hemulen said and continued on his way.

"Wait!" called Moomintroll. "Please explain . . ."

But the Hemulen didn't answer. He disappeared into the darkness, fretting just like everybody else about the arrival of Christmas.

The Moomins went inside the house to rummage for presents. Pappa selected his finest fishing rod.
He wrote "For Christmas" on a tag and tied it tightly to his gift.

Snorkmaiden took off her anklet, which was the most beautiful thing she owned. She sighed softly as she wrapped it up in tissue paper.

Mamma opened her top secret box and took out a book of beautiful paintings. It was the only book of its kind in all of Moominvalley.

Moomintroll's present was so secret and special that no one was allowed to see it. Even when winter was over and spring had come, he refused to tell anyone what he had given away.

They laid the presents out around the fir tree.

Then they sat down in the snow and waited for disaster to strike.

Time passed, but nothing happened.

Only the little creature dared to venture out again.
It had brought all its friends and relatives along,
a group of little woodies, toffles and creeps, all of whom
were equally small and grey and timid.

"Happy Christmas," whispered the creature, shyly.

"You're certainly the first to think Christmas is happy,"
said Moominpappa. "Aren't you afraid of what might
happen when it comes?"

"It's already here," peeped the little creature. "May
we take a look? You really do have the most wonderful
fir tree."

"And so much delicious food!" said one of its relatives.

"And real presents!" squeaked another.

The little woodies, toffles and creeps were sitting quite
still. They had never had a Christmas of their own. The
Moomin family could feel their longing grow stronger and
stronger. Eventually Moominmamma edged a little closer
to Pappa and whispered something to him.

Pappa reflected, then turned to the creatures and said:

"Help yourselves, it's all for you!"

The little creatures could hardly believe their ears.
Could the fir tree and the presents and the scrumptuous
food really all be for them? Their noses started twitching.
For once they could celebrate Christmas properly.

Still, the Moomin family thought it best to stay hidden
in the house. Christmas might be angry with them.

The Moomin family hid under the table in the drawing room, just in case. They stayed there for a long time and waited. Nothing happened.

Eventually they plucked up the courage to look out of the window.

Outside all the little creatures – the woodies, the toffles and the creeps – were celebrating Christmas. They were eating and drinking and opening presents. They had never had so much fun! Finally they climbed the fir tree and attached burning candles to all its branches.

"There ought to be a great big star at the top of the tree," said a little creature's uncle.

"Oh," whispered Moominmamma. "Apparently we were supposed to get a star as well. But how could we? The stars are so far away . . ."

They looked to the sky, which was bigger and blacker than anything, and saw thousands more glittering stars than there ever were in summer. And then they saw it: the biggest star of all was hanging directly above their fir tree.

"I'm sleepy now," said Moominmamma. "I'm tired of trying to figure out what all this is supposed to mean. But it certainly doesn't seem dangerous."

"I'm not afraid of Christmas any more," said Moomintroll with a yawn. "The Hemulen and Mrs Fillyjonk and everyone else must have misunderstood."

Then they all crawled into their beds and went back to sleep to wait for spring.

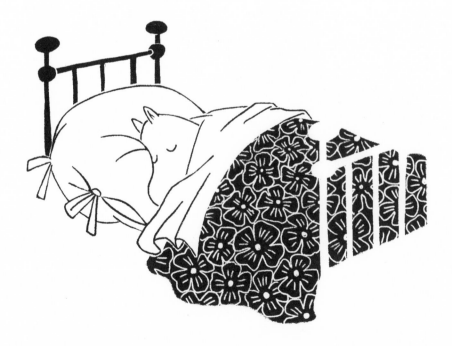

First published 2018 by Bonnier Carlsen Bokförlag, Stockholm
This edition published 2019 by Macmillan Children's Books
an imprint of Pan Macmillan
20 New Wharf Road, London, N1 9RR
Associated companies throughout the world
www.panmacmillan.com

ISBN: 978-1-5290-0363-5
© Moomin Characters ™

Written by Alex Haridi and Cecilia Davidsson
Illustrated by Filippa Widlund
Translated by A. A. Prime

1 3 5 7 9 8 6 4 2

A CIP catalogue record for this book is available from the British Library.

Printed in China